CAN ADULTS
BECOME HUMAN?

Think you can handle
another
Jamie Kelly diary?

#1 LET'S PRETEND THIS NEVER HAPPENED

#2 MY PANTS ARE HAUNTED!

#3 AM I THE PRINCESS OR THE FROG?

#4 NEVER DO ANYTHING, EVER

#5 CAN ADULTS BECOME HUMAN?

Coming soon . . .

#6 THE PROBLEM WITH HERE
IS THAT
IT'S WHERE I'M FROM

Jim Benton's Tales from Mackerel Middle School

DEAR DUMB DIARY,

CAN ADULTS BECOME HUMAN?

BY JAMIE KELLY

SCHOLASTIC INC.

New York   Toronto   London   Auckland   Sydney
Mexico City   New Delhi   Hong Kong   Buenos Aires

No part of this publication may be reproduced, stored in a retrieval system,
or transmitted in any form or by any means, electronic, mechanical,
photocopying, recording, or otherwise, without written permission of the
publisher. For information regarding permission, write to Scholastic Inc.,
Attention: Permissions Department, 557 Broadway, New York, NY 10012

ISBN 0-439-79621-0

Copyright © 2006 by Jim Benton
All rights reserved. Published by Scholastic Inc.
SCHOLASTIC, APPLE, and associated logos are trademarks
and/or registered trademarks of Scholastic Inc.

12 11 10 9 8 7 6 5 4 3 2   6 7 8 9 10 11/0
Printed in the U.S.A.   40
First Scholastic Printing, May 2006

For The Office Ladies,
most of whom
are really and truly nice.

Thanks to Mary K., Summer, and Griffin, who help more than anybody could ever imagine.

Thanks to Maria Barbo, who worked from afar, and Shannon Penney, who did her work from aclose.

Thanks also to Steve Scott, Susan Jeffers Casel, and Craig Walker.

And most of all, thanks to the DDD readers.

THIS DIARY PROPERTY OF

Jamie Kelly

SCHOOL: Mackerel Middle School

Locker: 101

Favorite Teacher: Miss Anderson

Favorite Animal: KOALA. Also dogs
But not smelly ones.

Most Hated candy of all time:
Butterscotch HARD CANDIES

A DECENT
HUMAN BEING
WOULD NEVER
READ ANOTHER
PERSON'S DIARY.

Dear Whoever is reading My Dumb Diary,

Are you sure you're supposed to be reading somebody else's diary? Maybe I told you that you could, so that's okay. But if you are Angeline, I did **NOT** give you permission, so stop it.

If you are my parents, then YES, I know I am not allowed to call people idiots and dopes or to talk about *gross bodily functions* and all that, but this is a *diary,* and I didn't actually "say" any of it. I *wrote* it. And, if you punish me for it, then I will know that you read my diary, which I am **not** giving you permission to do.

Now, by the power vested in me, I do promise that everything in this diary is true, or at least as true as I think it needs to be.

Signed, *Jamie Kelly*

PS: What kind of animal reads a person's diary, anyway?

PPS: Oh! I bet I know. I bet it's one of those big, dirty animals that eventually ends up on a bun with mustard and onions. Hint, hint.

And let's not forget what curiosity did to that cat...

Monday 02

Dear Dumb Diary,

TEACHERS DON'T FART.

I spend something like **eight months** a year, **seven hours** a day with teachers. If they did, I'd know it. Moms do it. Dads do it. Beagles do it (sometimes so bad that your eyes burn and your lungs might try to escape by jumping out your mouth).

Even *I* do it. One time I had a fart that lasted so long, that around the middle of the fart I was thinking back to when the fart began.

Anyway, I was thinking about teachers and their intestinal gas today in school and that may have prevented me from learning anything. Maybe the teachers just need to try harder. (To teach me things, that is. Not to cut one.)

SILENT BUT VIOLENT

Seriously though, it's hard for me to blame teachers. It's probably pretty tough to stand up in front of us normal human beings and try to convince us that the equator is interesting, or that the clothes that the people in Wheretheheckistan wear are beautiful. (Fashions in other countries sometimes appear to be based on one person daring another person to wear something in public.)

Fortunately, I do have one teacher who I always like: Miss Anderson, my art teacher. She's my **BTF**, which is like a **BFF** but it's for teachers. She is pretty enough to be a waitress, and she notices important things like when I create my own private glitter blends. (Currently, I'm using a secret mixture of gold, red, and magenta. It's pretty much magnificent.)

Art class would be perfect if Angeline (Miss Blondy BlondWad) wasn't in it. Angeline is not an artist and when she stands next to something, she has a way of making it look less pretty by comparison. Which, when you think about it, is a form of vandalism that sadly, our legal system has no penalty for yet.

see? she made the MONA LISA into some weird old lady with no eyebrows

Oh, and Mom **FINALLY** got me the shoes I wanted. Dad, being a dude, only has, like, two pairs of shoes and can't fully appreciate how much you can need a pair of shoes that you don't need at all.

Mom is totally immune to my begging for most things, but since she is a girl — or used to be one — she has way too many shoes and sympathizes with other females who also want too many shoes.

Anyway, they make me look 20 or something.

DAD'S HUGE SHOE ASSORTMENT

1. The pAIR He wears to work every DAY

2. The pAIR He WOULD WEAR TO SHOVEL BURNING MANURE IN THE RAIN.

Tuesday 03

Dear Dumb Diary,

My social studies teacher, Mr. VanDoy, never smiles. I know that's hard to believe, because everybody smiles about something, right?

Isabella smiles when her brothers get in trouble. Angeline smiles when she thinks about how much prettier she is than, like, a waterfall or a unicorn. I smile when I think about a unicorn kicking Angeline over a waterfall. But Mr. VanDoy doesn't smile at all. I wonder if when you become an adult, you can lose your sense of humor the way you lose your teeth or hair or fashion sense.

Our social studies class is studying animal social groups now, which means we are learning how ants and chimps and birds live together and tolerate one another. (Personally, I hate ants so much that even if I was an ant, I don't think I could resist stomping on myself.)

STOMP STOMP

SQUISH STOMP

Isabella says we can do our homework just by watching the educational channels, although it seems like every time I turn those on they are showing the footage of the cheetah running down the cute little antelope and not the stuff we need for class.

Isabella says that if she had been born a cute little antelope and saw the cheetah coming, she would just kick another cute little antelope in the shins so it couldn't run very fast, and the cheetah would get *it* instead of her.

Pretty smart, huh? Except I'm pretty sure that if Isabella had been born a cute little antelope, all the cute little antelopes in Africa would be hunting and eating cheetahs by now. As well as elephants and human beings. I really and truly don't think we're thankful often enough that Isabella was not born a cute little antelope.

On the subject of Isabella, I noticed her notice my new shoes today, and I'm sure I noticed her noticing how they make me look 20, but I also noticed her trying not to be noticed, so I did the polite thing and unnoticed her doing it, because that's what friends do.

Dumb Diary, did I ever tell you how Isabella and I became friends? It was instantaneous. It's what people call **Like at First Sight.** It was way back in second grade. On the first day of school, our teacher, Miss Baker, was asking us all to stand up and say our names. Isabella stood and said, "I'm Isabella Vinchella," and Lewis Clarke giggled.

It took three teachers and half the class to pull Isabella off Lewis, who she seemed to be playing like a fat little xylophone. (He actually made higher notes when she punched him in certain places.)

Violence is never the answer, of course, unless your question is "Hey Isabella, what's the answer?" But I admired the fact that she was like some sort of dangerous little mousetrap that you just should not stick your fingers in. I told her so, and she liked the description.

We became instant friends, and have been that way ever since — although sometimes Isabella seems less like a mousetrap and more like an atomic bomb that you should not stick your fingers in.

Wednesday 04

Dear Dumb Diary,

Today in art class, Miss Anderson asked us to give her ideas for our next assignment. I suggested that we make self-portraits with a lot of glitter and jewels. Angeline suggested collages (*ugh!*). Isabella suggested that we decorate padlocks to put on our bedroom doors so our brothers can't get in our stuff.

Although her judgment is usually excellent, this time Miss Anderson went with Angeline's suggestion of collages. I suspect this was because of some kind of law that says she has to offer a certain number of projects for **The Artistically Impaired** each year. Since not everybody in the world has what it takes to grow up to be an important artist like I might become if I decide not to be a scientist who also makes a lot of money dancing on TV, art teachers occasionally must offer projects that the kids who were born with toes for fingers can do — like collages. A collage is when you

my graceful hand

A toe-fingered person

cut things out of a magazine and glue them onto a piece of paper. These are not terribly challenging projects to complete.

Once on a field trip to a petting zoo, I saw this goat that had eaten a newspaper and some cotton candy and he had made his own little collages all over the barnyard. Really quite amazing work for a goat.

I would've gotten one, too, except that the teacher caught me putting some goat art in my lunch box.

STABBING ART
LUMP WITH
STICK

These collage projects wouldn't be so bad if Miss Anderson subscribed to a *variety* of magazines, but most of the old magazines she brings in have headlines like COOKING SMALL MEALS FOR ONE IS NOT NECESSARILY SAD or HEY! MAYBE DOGS ARE BETTER THAN HUSBANDS.

She also has a lot of bride magazines, but somebody has blacked out the teeth or drawn arrows through the heads of most of the pictures, which makes them useless unless your collage is about a kid that lives near a church and really likes archery but has super bad aim.

Isabella says the magazines mean that Miss Anderson is totally desperate to get a husband, which is odd because she is even more beautiful than Mrs. LaBeau down the street, who has already had five or six husbands by now. Isabella says that it means that Miss Anderson must do something so **BAD** that it outweighs her PRETTY. Helpfully, Isabella has the ratios all worked out.

Isabella said that Miss Anderson is pretty enough to eat salad for breakfast, let's say, but not pretty enough to brush her teeth with ketchup. Isabella also said that Angeline is pretty enough to brush her teeth with mustard, but not pretty enough to burn down SeaWorld.

Isabella said that she, herself, is pretty enough to put mayonnaise on her popcorn, but not pretty enough to burn down SeaWorld unless Angeline and Miss Anderson help her. Isabella says that *I'm* pretty enough to be an exhibit at SeaWorld. (I suspect she is jealous of my shoes. I'm telling you, they make me look 20 or something!)

I'm sure she meant a manatee

13

There was a time when I would not have known how to react to something like that from Isabella, but after being her friend all these years, it was perfectly clear to me what I had to do. . .

After that, Isabella spent most of the afternoon trying to remove the picture of the toothless, arrow-headed bride that I glued to her hair. Guess that makes us even.

I'm not sure how she finally got it out, but knowing Isabella, it could have been anything

Thursday 05

Dear Dumb Diary,

Okay. It turns out that you can't exactly get even with Isabella. I had forgotten about the time one of her mean older brothers ate a chocolate bar that she had been saving and she snuck into his room that night and quietly put an earthworm in his sleeping mouth and then taped it shut. One can hardly imagine his panic. Now her brother gets a little sick every time he sees candy, and *THAT* is what Isabella calls *"even."*

While it's true that THE EARTHWORMING was over chocolate and Isabella has a huge chocolate-dependency problem, Isabella can "Bring It" — as she likes to say — even when it's not about chocolate.

So, first thing this morning, she "brought it" to me, and I was called to go down to the office.

But let's be reasonable about placing blame here. Yes, Isabella told on me for gluing something to her, but the collage thing was Angeline's idea in the first place, so she really is mostly to blame for this.

I believe that there are schools with nice office ladies that are pretty and don't smell like discount coffee and butterscotch candies. In fact, it wouldn't surprise me to learn that **ALL** other schools are like that. Just not my school.

Now, to be fair, it's not just the office ladies. Many adults have a need to drink coffee all day so that they can remain alert and have bad breath.

But the candy is a different story. Our office ladies **ENJOY** being mean, especially to me, and a huge fishbowl of chocolate won't do that to you the way a huge fishbowl of butterscotch will. Here is why: Every time they look at the bowl, the office ladies think: "We could have bought good candy. We hate these hard butterscotch candies. Butterscotch candies aren't good for anything. I think we should take it out on the next kid who walks in here."

And that kid is usually me.

I wonder if every school has a CAULDRON in the office?

Isabella had told on me to Assistant Principal Devon, who wears ties but is nice, anyway. He said I shouldn't glue things in people's hair and **blah-blah** be kind to each other and **blah-blah** what kind of a world would this be if **blah-blah-blah**.

He was just getting ready to come up with some sort of punishment when I asked him what happened to his glasses — he used to have these **HUGE** glasses he could probably see molecules with — and he said that his niece talked him into getting eye surgery so he wouldn't need them anymore, which I have to admit was a pretty good idea, because without his glasses he looked almost handsome for an old guy (**He's probably forty!**). Not that I'm an expert on Isabella's newest **GOOD-LOOKING-ENOUGH FORMULA,** but I suppose that he is still not handsome enough to burn down SeaWorld. Though he *is* probably handsome enough to, let's say, step right on a fish.

Assistant Principal Devon slid his old glasses across the desk to me and asked if I wanted to try them on, which I did, but at that exact moment, one of the mean office ladies walked into his office and when I turned around and saw **Pure Ugliness** magnified a million jillion times, I screamed a little.

Pure Ugly was just never meant to be magnified that much.

I guess my scream startled the office lady enough to send her stumbling backward into a counter and knock over the big bowl of butterscotch candies. Now, I know this sounds pretty good, but it gets better because when she stepped on one of those little candies with her clunky ugly old shoes, her leg went right out from underneath her and her hip made a popping sound loud enough to be heard over my laughter.

Somebody called 911, and Assistant Principal Devon sent me back to class. As I went I could hardly believe that there was a time when I thought those butterscotch candies weren't good for anything.

Friday 06

Dear Dumb Diary,

Isabella apologized for telling on me. And I apologized for gluing a picture to her head. Isabella's apology went something like this: "It's your own fault, Jamie. You know how I roll, when it comes to getting even."

Not exactly the kind of thing you read inside a greeting card, I guess. But that's Isabella and that's how she rolls. One of these days I'm going to get a way to roll.

ISABELLA'S MOM

Also, her mom just started another diet, which means Isabella's whole house has to go on a diet, because that's how her mom's stomach rolls . . . when it comes to her mom's stomach rolls. And when Isabella has a sudden reduction in sugar intake, she is not her normal pleasant self.

I got high fives for attacking the mean office lady. Of course, I didn't really attack anybody. I would never attack anybody. Who wasn't blond. And Angeline.

But when a story travels through a middle school, it gets built up every time somebody tells somebody else. Like this one time when there was a rumor going around that Angeline was the prettiest girl in the state, which was totally wrong because somebody prettier could have been flying over the state in an airplane, and when you fly *over* a state technically you are *in* the state, so Angeline was not necessarily the prettiest. For a couple of hours.

I felt kind of bad about the **Injured Mean Office Lady** so I stopped by the office and asked Mr. Devon how she was. He said she broke her hip and will be retiring. I guess the office ladies place a lot of importance on hips since they seem to be having some sort of contest to grow the biggest pair.

Office chair designed just for our office LADIES.

The butterscotch candies were gone, and Mr. Devon didn't punish me for gluing Isabella's hair so I guess that means I'm pretty enough to break a Mean Office Lady's hip if a handsomish assistant principal and the second prettiest girl in the state help me do it. (Let's face it: Angeline's collage thing was the reason I was in the office in the first place. . . .)

ANGELINE SUGGESTED COLLAGES

WHICH MADE ME GLUE A PICTURE TO ISABELLA

WHICH MADE ISABELLA TELL ON ME

WHICH MADE THE ASSISTANT PRINCIPAL LEND ME HIS GLASSES

WHICH MADE THE OFFICE LADY SCARE ME

WHICH MADE ME SCREAM LOUD ENOUGH TO CAUSE A HIP ACCIDENT

SEE? ANGELINE'S FAULT, KIND OF

And Angeline, whose entire life is **One Continuous Walk Down the Runway**, managed to find time to say, "Good job on the office lady, Jamie. Couldn't have come at a better time. Let's hope her replacement is pretty."

Which, now that I think about it, is sort of weird, because why would Angeline care??

Unless she is planning — as I have always suspected — to do away with us all, one at a time, and replace us with more attractive versions of ourselves. And now she has made me an accomplice in her sinister plan.

REPLACEMENT ME ←

SHE'LL PROBABLY TAKE MY SHOES ↙

Here's the thing about Angeline. I know that she shouldn't really bother me that much. I mean, Angeline has even done nice things for me in the past, although I have come to believe that these were probably accidental.

There's just something so infuriating about perfect people. When's she's nice it makes me mad. When she's pretty, it makes me mad. It never changes. I guess the only good thing about Angeline is that she can never bother me more than she does right now. Perfect people make me perfectly ill. Hey, maybe that's how I roll.

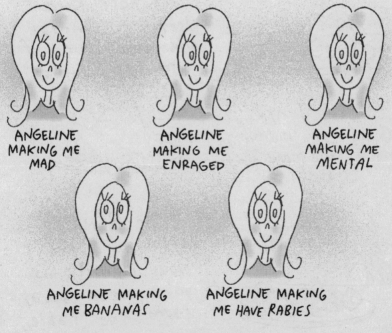

ANGELINE
MAKING ME
MAD

ANGELINE
MAKING ME
ENRAGED

ANGELINE
MAKING ME
MENTAL

ANGELINE MAKING
ME BANANAS

ANGELINE MAKING
ME HAVE RABIES

Aunt Carol called while we were eating tonight, which ticked Mom off a little, since she had spent all afternoon ruining dinner. But then she started talking to her and got all excited because Aunt Carol is going to be staying with us for a while. She's planning on moving to the area.

Mom hardly even noticed when Dad and I carefully concealed the uneaten portion of the meal with cleverly draped napkins and snuck them right past her and into the garbage. (Mom's cooking makes **Crafty Napkin Draping** an essential survival skill around here.)

"The Rose Blossom"
Useful to conceal one deadly lump of grossness within.

"The Tent"
Good for hiding a more massive icky OBJECT.

"The BANDITO"
Useful to conceal your identity as you sneak away from the table.

Aunt Carol is my mom's younger sister, so when I look at her, I think I can imagine my mom before she became afflicted with **Momness**. (Or would that be called Momism? Momitis? Anyway, there's no cure.)

Aunt Carol is single, so her wardrobe is similar to the clothes my old Barbies used to have except that Aunt Carol doesn't spend as much time up on her tiptoes.

I love my mom, of course, and if she was anything like Aunt Carol, I probably would have liked her before she became an adult, but as you know, Dumb Diary, adults are very hard to like except for people in the entertainment business — with the exception of clowns, who may be the hardest of all.

SOME OF THE WORST TYPES OF ADULTS

GROUCHY OLD MEAN TURD GUY

LADY WHO THINKS SHE'S BETTER THAN EVERYBODY

CLOWN WITH DIRTY CLOTHES

CLOWN'S FRIEND WHO IS ALSO A CLOWN

Saturday 07

Dear Dumb Diary,

Isabella came over today. We had a little mini-project to do for social studies. Our teacher, Mr. VanDoy (who never smiles) told us to try to find social behavior in people that was similar to the social behavior in animals.

Isabella does not usually volunteer to kill a Saturday by coming over to do homework, but there still are no sweets in her house, and we're always pretty well stocked with junk.

Mr. VanDoy showed us a video last week with chimpanzees and he told us about all the complicated ways they communicate, but after seeing a bunch of monkeys on the educational channels, I really think that most communication between monkeys is just them saying: "Dude. What's wrong with your butt? Did you back into a fan or something? Did you sit down on the stove? Do you need to go to the hospital? There's something wrong with your butt."

Once we started talking about it, I started seeing lots of ways that adults are like animals.

My dad goes to an office every day, and the building is like a beehive where the little adults scurry around and make honey and have to do what the queen bee says, although in my dad's case the queen is a man bee — and they don't make honey, they make accounting.

My mom is sort of like a lioness that prowls the grasslands, instinctively hunting a microwavable zebra for her family because it takes too long to prepare a real zebra.

And Isabella . . .

And this is where it broke down for us. We could see how adults were like animals, but we really couldn't find any examples of how *we* were like animals.

Isabella says that science believes that adults might not even actually be human beings. And the more we talked about it, the righter she seemed.

They are LARGE AND GROSSLY HAIRY.

when they sing along to their favorite songs, many sound like a Hog Being Dragged by its tail.

They are capable of doing mindless activities for hours on end.

After exercising, many acquire an interesting camel-like Fragrance.

They just can't seem to resist SLOBBERING ALL OVER YOU

Sunday 08

Dear Dumb Diary,

   HOORAY! Aunt Carol came today. This really threw Dad's Sunday off because he has a lot of important things to do on Sunday, like dress like a slob and halfway complete a project around the house.

   But he always manages to look presentable when Mom's relatives come over . . . although he often looks like something itches.

DAD TRYING NOT TO THINK ABOUT HOW MUCH HE'D RATHER BE IN SWEATPANTS

Technically, Aunt Carol is an adult relative, and normally, this would be a big problem, since most conversations with adult relatives sound like this:

OLD RELATIVE: So, how's school?

ME: Fine.

OLD RELATIVE: And how's soccer going?

ME: Fine. (If I explain that I've never played soccer, it will just lead to extra questions.)

OLD RELATIVE: So how do you like all this rain we're having?

ME: I don't know.

But Aunt Carol is a bit more fun:

AUNT CAROL: So, how's school going?

ME: Fine.

AUNT CAROL: Are any of the kids really gross?

MOM: Stop it, Carol.

ME: Angeline is gross.

MOM: Jamie!

AUNT CAROL: Did you know your mom wet her pants once at school?

MOM: Don't listen to her, Jamie. She's taken her allergy medicine, and she doesn't know what she's saying (whispers something really angry at Aunt Carol).

AUNT CAROL: Jeez! Okay, okay. I'll drop it. Uh, Jamie, uh . . . How do you like all this rain we're having?

ME: I don't know.

AUNT CAROL: I'll bet your mom hates it. It could get her pants wet.

This is the point at which Mom throws something at Aunt Carol and the conversation is pretty much over. It's really hard not to like somebody that can make your mom throw a pillow.

It's because they're sisters. Mom says that nobody, anywhere, can ever make you crazy like a relative. Not a friend, not an enemy, **NOBODY.**

It's like my one dirty small cousin with the strawberry allergy, who is a big wad of filth and a dope. He drives me nuts, but at least he's useful at family gatherings because when I stand next to him, I appear clean and lovely and bright in comparison — not that I'm not clean and lovely and bright — but he just makes me look so much lovelier and cleaner and brighter.

I think Isabella could also testify to the **Problem with Relatives,** as could her mean brother, **Old Worm-Swallower.**

Dear Dumb Diary,

Are you even *allowed* to re-tell on somebody? See, Isabella knows that Mr. Devon forgot to punish me for gluing a picture to her head, and so she **dropped him a note** reminding him. *SHE RE-TOLD.* You can't re-tell on somebody, can you?

I was pretty angry about it when I was called down to the office *again* to get lectured about the dangers of getting something glued to you and how not gluing things to each other was the glue that held society together, or whatever Assistant Principal Devon was going to say this time. (It's still my shoes, isn't it, Isabella? They make me look 20 or something.)

Does the ENTIRE WORLD RESENT MY SHOES?

COULD YOU BLAME THEM?

We're missing a mean office lady now, of course, and the other **Mean Office Ladies** were out pricing a new cauldron or something, so I just walked right into Assistant Principal Devon's office, only to see the unmistakably glorious back of Angeline's flawless blond head. For a moment I found myself fantasizing about all of the terrific punishments Angeline might be getting.

COLOR OF EYES MEDICALLY CHANGED FROM BABY BLUE TO BABY BARF

GLORIOUS MANE OF SILKEN GOLD REPLACED WITH COARSE TUFT OF BRISTLES FROM WARTHOG BUTT.

NO LONGER ALLOWED TO GO BY LOVELY NAME OF "ANGELINE." NOW HER OFFICIAL LEGAL NAME IS SOMETHING LIKE "CANKER SORE" OR "SMEAR."

WART PIE

But suddenly she turned around and she was wearing Assistant Principal Devon's old glasses, which magnified the **Pure Beauty** of her eyes (the exact same color as a blue Popsicle) about a million jillion times, and this time I screamed a little because **Pure Beauty** was just never meant to be magnified that much, either.

My scream made her scream and I stumbled backward into the same counter that took out the Mean Office Lady. As a self-trained ballerina, I would have easily recovered, except that these new shoes are a little slippery on the bottom, and I took it right in the head.

Next thing I knew, they had given me **The Small Cold Thing** to put on my head. **The Small Cold Thing** is the absolute highest form of medical treatment they can give you at school — it's practically their version of a heart transplant — so I guess I must have hit my head hard enough to nearly take it off.

They called my mom to come get me, but Aunt Carol came instead. I have to say, Dumb Diary, that Assistant Principal Devon and Aunt Carol sure were not weeping and wringing their hands fretfully the way I would expect to be wept and wrung over while I was almost dying. In fact, they seemed to be sort of — but this can't be true — *chitchatting*.

Ugh! EMERGENCY!!!!! Have to stop writing. Stinker ate something Mom made yesterday and, believe it or not, Mom's cooking actually smells even worse when you run it through the antique digestive system of an old fat beagle. Must . . . make . . . it . . . to . . . door . . . eyes . . . burning. . . .

I'm not sure if she's going to make it. She inhaled a LOT of PURE DOG STINK.

BUT THANK GOODNESS SHE LEFT A NOTE NOT TO PUT TUBES IN HER NOSE. THOSE ARE TOTALLY GROSS-LOOKING.

Tuesday 10

Dear Dumb Diary,

I had to sleep on the couch last night because Stinker committed that **Odor Crime** in my room and even though Mom would usually just make me sleep in there, anyway, I pointed out that the combination of **Beagle Fumes** and my head injury could be disastrous. I told her about this one girl I heard of from a different school that was camping and had to spend the entire night in a tent with an eleven-year-old poodle that had eaten four burritos. When they found her the next morning, she was just a little pile of ash. I might have made part of that up, but Mom let me sleep on the couch, and since I was downstairs I heard my Aunt Carol roll in around 11:30 and talk to my mom in the kitchen while I expertly pretended to be asleep.

Pretending to be asleep is just about the best way to eavesdrop as long as you do it well. Don't scrunch your eyes closed too hard, and don't snore like they do in cartoons.

I couldn't hear them very well, but it was all made painfully clear to me this morning when Aunt Carol drove me to school and **PARKED THE CAR!** This afforded me an early morning look at Miss Bruntford (the lunchroom monitor) because she also monitors the parking lot in the morning, and is there to helpfully tell people exactly where they can't park. This is earlier than I had ever planned to look at Bruntford, and it was not agreeing with my Crunchberries. But it got worse.

"Guess what, Jamie?" Aunt Carol says all happy in that voice that makes you worry because when adults are this happy you should worry. "Dan — I mean — Assistant Principal Devon offered me a job that just opened up in the office. I'm going to work at your school. Isn't that great?"

AUNT CAROL AFFLICTED WITH TYPICAL ADULT DUMBNESS —

Aunt Carol, Aunt Carol, Aunt Carol.
(I'm slowly shaking my head sadly as I write this
part.) There was a time when you would have
understood that a person would rather bathe in a
tub of hot dog slobber than have a relative of theirs
working at their school. But it looks like you're **ONE
OF THEM** now. Aunt Carol, you're an **Adult**.

"Yes," I lied, realizing that I was lying to Aunt
Carol for maybe the first time ever, so I added, "And
I'm not lying to you."

ADULTNESS

COULD IT
HAPPEN
TO SOMEBODY
CLOSE TO
YOU?

In social studies today, Isabella asked Mr. VanDoy (who never smiles) if there were any animals that would eat their own nieces. (I had told Isabella all about Aunt Carol taking a job at the school.) He listed a whole bunch — mostly the mean animals like crocodiles and sharks — but he said that among the higher primates, like chimps, the relationship between aunts and nieces is particularly close, too close, I would imagine, for an aunt chimp to take an office job at her niece chimp's school.

Poor Aunt Carol (again with the sad, sad head-shaking). She's not even a monkey anymore.

Wednesday 11

Dear Dumb Diary,

Isabella asked me today how Assistant Principal Devon had punished me on Monday. Isabella has already demonstrated that she is a RE-teller, so I had to make her believe I was punished. Because Isabella has mean older brothers, she is an expert on lying. Once, Isabella had convinced a lunch lady that she had been diagnosed with a cake deficiency by her doctor, and was medically entitled to an extra dessert. This may not sound like much, but lunch ladies are very sharp, especially in the extra-dessert department, and talking one out of cake is the type of thing people write folk songs about.

So I said right back to her, "What do *you* think he did?"

See, by doing this, I got Isabella to sort of tell me the lie she would believe.

"Detention?" she said.

"Yup," I said. "I got detention."

Ha-ha! Fooled you, Isabella!

Thursday 12

Dear Dumb Diary,

Okay. You cannot fool Isabella that easily.

I must have sounded a little too happy, or too sad, or that lie detector she has built into her butt was going off, but she did not buy it, and she re-told *AGAIN*. And *AGAIN* I was sent down to see Assistant Principal Devon, and now, even worse, my Aunt Carol would be there.

But the office was unlike any office I had ever been in. The office ladies were **SMILING**. There was some music playing softly. There were some flowers, and in the spot where the butterscotch candies used to be was a great big dish full of little chocolate candy bars.

43

In the center of this transformed office was my Aunt Carol. And when she saw me she waved and grinned and said, "Jamie! Hi, Jamie! Everybody, this is my niece, Jamie."

The Mean Office Ladies took those ugly things they keep on the fronts of their heads (where a face would normally go) and SMILED at me with them. I had never thought it possible.

Then, Assistant Principal Devon came out of his office and showed me Isabella's latest memo.

"Your aunt has told me about your friend, Isabella. She's a **re-teller**. I figure she's going to keep re-telling until you get punished, so how about this?" He dropped her note on the floor. "How about if you pick that up and toss it in the wastebasket? Then you can tell her I made you clean the office."

Amazing, right? His solution was kind of a lie *and* kind of the truth at the same time.

I've heard that if you made a monkey bang on a keyboard long enough, it would eventually write *Romeo and Juliet*. This means that even a monkey might accidentally do something that appears human, and I think that's what Assistant Principal Devon was doing.

Only kids know how to tell the truth and tell a lie at the same time, but Assistant Principal Devon actually did it right in front of my very eyes.

So I smiled, picked up the note, and tossed it in the wastebasket before they ran out of candy bars, or the music stopped, or this monkey stopped banging on the keyboard.

Are ADULTS JUST DIM-WITTED BEASTS?

YES.

(unless an adult is reading this right now, in which case the answer is NO.)

Friday 13

Dear Dumb Diary,

Mom said that Aunt Carol is going to have a few people over in a couple weeks. Mom called it a party, but of course, since **adults** are not fully formed human beings, it's not a real party.

Aunt Carol was talking to Mom about some big date tonight, which was so gross to listen to that it was all I could do to keep eavesdropping. But they stopped talking when they discovered me casually crouching outside the kitchen, and they would not tell me whom this big gross date was with.

Aunt Carol is attractive enough to be a bank teller, but she is almost as old as my mom, so her date could be with anybody who is:

A) More attractive than she is, but dumber.
B) Less attractive than she is, but funnier.
C) The exact same level of attractiveness, but shorter.
D) The owner of a hot car.

Since I can't rely on Stinker to help me when I need him, I secretly fed him a can of beans at dinner so that he could again stink up my room in time for me to sleep on the couch.

Now all I have to do is wait until the beagle lets one fly.

POOF

And remember to be careful where I stand.

Saturday 14

Dear Dumb Diary,

Seriously, how selfish do you have to be to withhold your odor from somebody? Stinker stubbornly refused to gas me last night so I couldn't be down on the couch when Aunt Carol came home and eavesdrop about her date.

Mom and Aunt Carol left early to go shopping for Mom's appetizer stuff. My mom is an awful cook and everybody knows it: my family, my friends, the paramedics who had to come and save Dad from a lasagna once. But what some people don't know is that she *can* make appetizers. And she loves to demonstrate her skills to people.

And not just those little cocktail weenies or frozen pizza rolls. She makes fantastically delicious little tiny things that people can hardly believe she made. It's like Mom would be a great cook if she only had to prepare meals for Barbies. She'll be on full alert to keep us out of them. Especially Stinker, who has been known to bite guests in the thigh to make them drop one.

Since Mom was gone, Dad decided to get a jump on the **Projects** he doesn't finish on Sunday, by not finishing them today.

I called Isabella to come over and watch the educational channels but she was shopping with her mom.

DAD'S PROJECTS TODAY

1. Try to find hammer.

2. Try to fix wobbly table leg.

3. Try to teach neighborhood forty new swear words.

Sunday 15

Dear Dumb Diary,

Aunt Carol and I hung around a little today. And it was cool because I felt that we were once again as close as those aunt and niece chimpanzees without any butt problems that VanDoy has us studying. We walked down by the park, and there were some guys there that were about her age.

"I think those guys are checking me out," she said, which was cute, you might think, but as she is my aunt it was actually fairly sickening. I don't think I ever thought of Aunt Carol as being somebody that the guys would check out. I didn't think anybody that old was checking out anything except maybe books from the library on subjects like **Learning to Live with Those HUMONGOUS MOLES ON YOUR BACK.**

WARNING
ADULTS GET MAD
IF YOU PLAY
DOT-TO-DOT
ON THEIR
DEFORMITIES

When I was a kid, I used to think that I would never be ten years old — **A Double Digit, the Big One Oh** — But then it happened. *I turned ten* and I realized that ten wasn't that old. Sure, getting around was a little harder, going up stairs and stuff like that, but I still felt like a nine-year-old inside.

I wonder how old you are when people start checking you out. I wonder how old you are when they stop checking you out. I wonder if they really were checking her out. Or maybe she was checking them out. More than that, I wonder exactly how you perform a checking out, and how you receive one. I'm going to make Stinker check me out and try to see how I look in the mirror while he does it. **Shut up.** It's not weird to force your beagle to check you out. Probably lots of people do it.

Here's How Stinker did it. Is This Right?

Monday 16

Dear Dumb Diary,

You remember Bruntford, don't you Dumb Diary? She is the water buffalo that somebody trained to be a cafeteria monitor and whose job it is to make sure that everything in the lunchroom flows as smoothly as gravy through a grandma.

Ugh! I think I just grossed myself out a little. I'm for sure off gravy for a while.

OK. That was the ABSOLUTE LAST TIME I will ever use that description.

Anyway, it was your basic lunch scene. Me and Izzy was in the Hizzy, which means that I was there with Isabella. Although I'm not sure if it's cool for me to talk that way, but I like to so I only do it privately here in the Old Dumb Diary because it takes a lot of time to recover from a CRIME AGAINST COOLNESS.

DIZZY

KOAZZLE

TYRIZZLE ASAURIZZY RIZZLE REXLE

Like Isabella told me about this one girl that was ACTUALLY WITNESSED WITH HER ACTUAL FINGER IN HER ACTUAL NOSE. Look: I think that everybody puts a finger in his or her nose sometime, and what a finger and nose do voluntarily in private is nobody's business. But Isabella says that even though this girl was beautiful, she was not beautiful *enough* to publicly commit the *THIRD-WORST KNOWN FINGER CRIME* in public, (don't even ask me about one and two) and thirty years later she was in prison for stealing a car.

YOU'D PROBABLY HAVE TO BE A MOVIE STAR AND HOLDING TWO PUPPIES TO GET AWAY WITH FINGER CRIME NUMBER 3

Back to the Cafeteria: Bruntford, Isabella, the Hizzy, remember?

I was just minding my own business, walking in that way where technically you're walking, but you're almost running, but not really running. (We are not allowed to run in school.)

Angeline said, "Hey Jamie," which surprised me because Angeline and I are not friends and can never be friends because she was born with the deformity of being all perfect.

But I looked, anyway, possibly because I was curious to see how much I hated her at that exact moment, and when I looked, I slipped on something.

I'm not saying it was a blob of hair conditioner, but Angeline — a known abuser of hair conditioner — was in the vicinity, and all of my hours watching detectives on TV has taught me that the villain often lingers around the crime scene.

I'm not saying it was meat loaf, but cafeteria meat loaf is greasy enough to qualify as an industrial-grade lubricant, and some of it could easily have fallen from between those ugly flaps beneath Bruntford's nose. I think she calls them "lips."

I'm not saying it was my new shoes (they make me look 20 or something) but when I slammed into Bruntford, I was going about 20 or something.

So fast, in fact, that I think I may have actually **PLUNGED** into Bruntford a little. It was kind of like going underwater. You know, like when the sound changes and you're weightless.

But then I plopped out of the me-shaped indentation I had made in her, and the next thing I knew, I was in the office again, preparing the excuse that was going to go in my permanent record.

Aunt Carol is there in the office now, of course, which I figured meant that Mom would hear about it even sooner.

I could imagine the scene pretty clearly. She'd be all, "Jamie smashed into Bruntford today and got stuck in her a little, and it's one of the main things that indicates that she will probably steal cars and go to prison someday. Also it's going to cost a lot of money to get the indentation smoothed out of Bruntford."

But that's not what happened. All Aunt Carol did was read the note that Bruntford had given me, smile, and say "Slow down, hotshot." And then she **THREW IT IN THE TRASH**!! Just like that. The offense had been erased.

Almost like a MIRACLE!

"Don't you have to tell Assistant Principal Devon?" I whispered, as I knew we were doing crime.

"I'll tell him. It's fine. Don't worry," she said, and she winked the same wink that Mom winks when she's going to make something magically disappear before Dad finds out — like the time I used his electric razor to make Chihuahuas out of all my stuffed animals.

That's exactly what they look like when you shave them.

I thought about this all day; my aunt's power to make teachers' notes vanish, and I decided to never ever *ever* reveal it to Isabella. If Isabella knew that I had this awesome ability, there is no telling what she might do.

For Her Own Good, and That of Humanity, I do hereby SWEAR to NEVER TELL ANY OF THIS TO ISABELLA.

Tuesday 17

Dear Dumb Diary,

I told Isabella all of it.

I know, I may have said that I might not
tell her, but I couldn't hold out any longer. And it
was the right thing to do, because I really don't
think that she will ever try to take advantage of
it because all she did was smile a little and then
mutter something and twist her hands together,
and that does not **NECESSARILY** mean anything
sinister.

I've seen
Isabella's
Baby
pictures.
She was
born in
this
position

At lunch today, while Isabella and I were discussing just who at our school should be crated up and dropped on an island far, far away, Angeline, who coincidentally was the first one we had crated up, squirmed over to me and did that thing where somebody grabs you by the shoulders and makes little stampy stomps and shakes their head around and squeals those happy, giggly, shrill sounds that make puppies pee. You sort of feel like you've been playfully mauled by a really adorable grizzly. I don't know what this maneuver is called, but until you've had Angeline commit it against you, you probably don't realize that it could easily kill a person who was not prepared for it. **Homicide by Happiness? Gigglecide?**

SHAKE
SHAKE
SHAKE
SHAKE
SHAKE
SHAKE

WHIP
WHIP
WHIP
WHIP
GIGGLE
GIGGLE
SQUEALL
STAMPY
STAMPY
STAMP

Fortunately, but with no explanation, Angeline released me and ran off. Just like that. I wondered if I could tell on her for it. I mean, she did get her hair all over me. Assault with a fragrant weapon, maybe?

As I tried to formulate the appropriate accusation, across the cafeteria, I saw something **MUCH** stranger. I saw Aunt Carol talking to Miss Bruntford. This alone would have been cause for alarm, but then I saw Bruntford attempt to execute what I truly think may have been . . .

Is that even possible? Angeline, of course, is as weightless as a fairy, and her lustrous hair lustrously lusters all over the place in slow motion, but Bruntford clearly does not have that relationship with the earth's gravity. Bruntford may even have her own personal gravity. I would not be surprised to one day see a normal-sized cafeteria monitor in orbit around Bruntford.

But it was clear: Bruntford attempted the tiny little stamps. She tried flipping her head back and forth a little. She even made a squealy sound to make puppies pee, but coming out of her, I think it was directed more at jackal puppies. This was **Gigglecide**, and she was committing it against my Aunt Carol. Was she imitating human behavior the way a giant chimp in an ugly dress might? Mr. VanDoy did say that animals sometimes imitate human beings. . . .

When I turned to look at Isabella, I could tell that she had seen the whole thing, and a smile crept across her face like the thin wet track of a creeping snail.

Oh man, I think I grossed myself out again.

Other ways I have grossed myself out.

LOOKED UP NOSE WITH MIRROR AND FLASHLIGHT. (GROSSED OUT FOR 3 HOURS.)

CONVINCED MYSELF THAT SPAGHETTI LOOKED LIKE VEINS.

(GROSSED OUT ON SPAGHETTI FOR 4 MONTHS)

FORGOT TO LOOK AWAY WHEN PARENTS KISSED (STILL GROSSED OUT BUT IT ALSO MAKES ME LAUGH A LITTLE)

Wednesday 18

Dear Dumb Diary,

Miss Anderson was late for art class today. She was even prettier than her normal prettiness, which is as pretty as a waitress. Today, she might have been as pretty as an ice-skater or maybe even a circus lady.

She looked over our collages today, but she hardly noticed any of the details.

In fact, all Miss Anderson really wanted to do was get us on to our next assignment, which was her weirdest one in quite some time: to make a valentine card, but don't put anybody's name on it. It's not even close to Valentine's Day. Then she gave me a wink and said, "I'm counting on you, Jamie," which made sense, because I can make a valentine that would make an ant fall in love with an aardvark.

YOU ARE SO LOVELY THAT I WILL NOT SNORK YOU UP MY NOSE

But then she also winked at Angeline, who had just turned in her barf-pile of a collage. **AS IF** Angeline understood even the basics of **Valentinology**. Seriously. Angeline can do a lot of things, but her glittering skills are strictly amateur. Don't even get me started on her cotton-balling technique. I think that maybe Angeline is trying to steal my favorite teacher from me. Can you do that? Leave it to Angeline to come up with a brand-new kind of crime.

OTHER CRIMES SHE COMMITS

ASSAULT WITH INTENT TO DO BODILY CHARM

RECKLESS EYELASHERY

BEING SUPER GORGEOUS AND SMART SIMULTANEOUSLY

(I THOUGHT WE HAD ALL AGREED TO ONLY DO THESE ONE AT A TIME)

Isabella apologized for re-telling the second time. Which would make it **re-re-telling**. I know it was a sincere apology this time, because I know she sincerely wants to take advantage of Aunt Carol's ability to make teacher notes sincerely disappear. She also admitted that she was sincerely jealous of my shoes (they make me look 20 or something). At first she thought they were ugly, but when she realized how much I liked them, she decided she loved/resented them as well. So she even bought a pair when she was at the mall with her mom. Wasn't that nice of her?

We should cut her some slack. Going without sugar is really hard on Isabella. Yesterday, she even tried making an Oreo out of a couple crackers and some toothpaste.

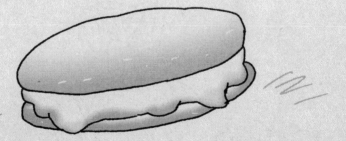

Aunt Carol wasn't at dinner tonight. When I asked Mom what was up, she said, "Nothing," but she said it in that real fast way that lets you know she was waiting for you to ask.

She said that Aunt Carol was out on a date again but she wouldn't tell me with whom.

Watching Mom make her appetizers all day has been making Stinker extra hungry, so it was easy to get him to eat baked beans again, in hopes that he would gas me out of my room so I could sleep on the couch and listen in when Aunt Carol got home. But Stinker is still stubbornly refusing to perform an odor, even when I gently sit down on him with all my weight, so I think I'm going to have to sleep in my room and not find out who the date was with.

Thursday 19

Dear Dumb Diary,

Isabella and I were eating lunch today.
Meat loaf. Meat loaf is what they always do to us on Thursday. They've tried to dress it up in the past, but it always comes down to this: chopped-up cow, made more appetizing by shaping it like a brick.

Some of the MEAT LOAF MAKEOVERS they've tried on us

MEAT LOAF CONES

CARVED INTO LOBSTER SHAPES

LOLLYLOAFS

Isabella and I were complaining about it to each other when Isabella got an idea. She stood up with her tray and told me to follow her and we walked right up to the trash where Bruntford was standing. Isabella looked Bruntford right in the eye and slid the uneaten meat loaf into the garbage. Then she grabbed my tray, did the same thing, and waited.

Dumping uneaten meat loaf in the garbage in front of Bruntford is a level of taunting that even rodeo clowns wouldn't dare. Isabella's mean older brothers have forced her to learn to stand her ground even when she is afraid, so Isabella and Bruntford held each other's stare for what seemed like a full minute until Bruntford eventually looked away and Isabella smiled.

THE BEST RODEO CLOWN that ever LIVED

"Your Aunt Carol has some sort of calming effect on Bruntford," Isabella said. "It's like when they put a little goat into a stall with a jumpy horse." Isabella also said that because of this we can do anything we want now and she proved her point by drinking as much water from the water fountain as she could hold. I told her that I didn't think there were any limits on the water, anyway, and she said, "Not anymore, Jamie. Not for us."

Eventually, Isabella was less thrilled about unlimited water

SLOSH

SLOSH SLOSH

Friday 20

Dear Dumb Diary,

Before class today, we asked Mr. VanDoy (the teacher who never smiles) about Isabella's idea that a goat could have a calming effect on a horse.
He said yes, which surprised me, because often teachers don't know as much as Isabella, and many have not heard of the things that Isabella knows to be true.

VAN DOY, WHO NEVER SMILES →

But impressively, may know as much as Isabella.

I was thinking about this, and the evidence that adults are animals, when **The Unpleasantness** occurred. Now, before I tell you about **The Unpleasantness**, Dumb Diary, you should know that I was not trying to get in trouble. It just sort of happened.

Here is a transcript of the exchange:

ISABELLA: So, what sort of animals are we learning about today, Mr. VanDoy?

VANDOY: I'm not quite sure. I've been very busy at home and I got a little behind.

ME: It doesn't look so little to me.

It happened so fast that I hardly knew I had said it. Isabella's huge whooping laugh and calls of **"Oh no, you dinnit"** did not help things, and Mr. VanDoy sent me with a note, to the office.

well c'mon.
it doesn't.

Not a problem, right? Aunt Carol will know what to do. Right? Except that when I got there, Aunt Carol was nowhere to be seen. Only the office ladies were there, and even though they all actually smiled at me with real smiles (not the ones they used to give me that looked like small rips in upholstery) they were *not* going to make the note go away.

I was surprised to see Miss Anderson walk out of Assistant Principal Devon's office. She was looking as pretty as ever, maybe even prettier, but not at all happy.

"He's all yours," she said and jabbed her thumb toward his office in a way that made me think she wished she was jabbing it toward his eye.

I gave Assistant Principal Devon the note from Mr. VanDoy, and he seemed to be holding back a laugh. Adults do that a lot, which is strange because who doesn't like to laugh? He said to choose my words more carefully in the future and it wouldn't hurt to apologize to Mr. VanDoy and not mention the size of his behind anymore.

He threw the note in the trash and as my eye followed it, I saw a **VALENTINE** in the trash. It was *MY* **valentine**. The one I had made in art. (My private glitter blend is impossible to mistake.)

It said, "**How about lunch?**" on it in Miss Anderson's gorgeous handwriting.

Miss Anderson used my valentine to ask Assistant Principal Devon to lunch? Can you imagine? I'm so flattered. Take that, Angeline! Miss Anderson is still *MY* BTF.

I'm guessing he said no and that's why she seemed angry. But here's the weird part: Miss Anderson and Assistant Principal Devon have worked together for years. Why would she give him a valentine now all of a sudden? Why would he say no? Why didn't my **glitterification skills** and **private blend** do the trick?

It's a mystery, all right.

mystified glitter artist →

GLORIOUS TRASHED VALENTINE ↓

How about Lunch?

PS: Gave Stinker beans again. I just know he's holding back on me. How selfish can you get?

Saturday 21

Dear Dumb Diary,

Mom says that since Aunt Carol is having her little party at our house next Friday, and my room is where they throw everybody's coats, I should start cleaning my room now. The process usually takes about five days. I don't like cleaning my room, but it is interesting to excavate down and find evidence of earlier Jamie civilizations buried deep beneath the visible mantle of junk.

DIRTY CLOTHES, RECENT MAGAZINES

REJECTED SHOE DEPOSIT ; LAYER OF HOBBIES I WAS INTERESTED IN FOR ABOUT 2 MINUTES

THINGS I THOUGHT I LOST IN KINDERGARTEN

MY OLD BABY BOTTLES AND TEETHING TOYS

COMPOST

FOSSILS

OIL

Sunday 22

Dear Dumb Diary,

Aunt Carol and I hung around today for a while. We talked about her job, which she says she "*LUUUVS*." She says she loves the school and the people she works with, and me, and the people she works with, and the whole wide world, and the people she works with.

ADULTS ARE DISTURBING WHEN THEY **LUV** something

I filled her in about some of the people she works with, since she's only been there a couple weeks, and adults — like animals — must know the way their little herds operate.

I told her that the office ladies used to be mean, but now they're nice and I think it's because Aunt Carol has substituted their hard butterscotch candies with chocolate, or maybe she is also a calming goat to them the way she is to Bruntford.

I told her that Mr. Evans, who is my English teacher, has a vein in his head that he can throb at you when he's angry but, like a bull elephant, he's more likely to just try to scare you than gore you.

I told her that Miss Anderson gave Assistant Principal Devon a valentine I had created while she was out of the office the other day in the way that a bird might offer another bird a big fat grub with glitter on it as part of a courtship ritual.

Aunt Carol got all flustered and angry and I can only assume it's because she is strongly against birds.

I mean, I'm no big fan myself, but c'mon, Aunty C.

Here's how she changed.

Maybe she's against valentines?

Monday 23

Dear Dumb Diary,

Aunt Carol drove me to school today and Bruntford was out patrolling the parking lot the way she does when she's not patrolling the lunchroom.

Aunt Carol stopped and talked to her while I went into school. This isn't the first time I've seen them talking. I can only assume that Bruntford was telling her to park somewhere else or finish her meat loaf or some other dumb Bruntford thing like that.

Bruntford also prowls the school parking lot. Or is this called skulking?

Later that day, Angeline did it again. **Gigglecide.** The stamping, the flailing, the puppy-pee squeals.

"The glasses!!!!!!!!!!!!!!!!! She slipped!!!!!!!!!!!!!!!!!!!!!!!!!!!! Your aunt!!!!!!!!!!!!!!!!!!!! She was mad at first . . . but . . . eeeee!!!!! This Friday!!!!!!!!!!" (I am not exaggerating the number of exclamation points here.) And all I could do was try to defend myself from getting strangled by Angeline's mop of flawless silken golden silky hair in the way you might have to wrestle a massive octopus that smelled like Green Apple shampoo.

Why is Angeline doing this?

I COULD HAVE BEEN MAIMED BY A FLYING EXCLAMATION POINT

I asked Mom what she thought about Angeline but she was concentrating too hard on her precious appetizers and stepping on Stinker to keep him from jumping up on the table to even hear what I had asked. All she could say was, "I like Angeline. She's a nice girl." That was all I needed to hear to know that she had no idea who I was talking about.

MOMS CAN FEND OFF UP TO THREE FAT DOGS WITHOUT INTERRUPTING THEIR WORK

Tuesday 24

Dear Dumb Diary,

Isabella got in trouble **EIGHT TIMES TODAY**. She kept doing things just bad enough to get sent to Assistant Principal Devon, but not serious enough for the teacher to call the police.

Isabella's rap sheet:

- Told Mrs. Palmer, the science teacher, that biology is the study of everything that is too gross to go into any other "ology" and that's why she teaches it.
- Ran in the hallway.
- Drew unflattering picture of Mr. Evans on his chalkboard. (Which alone might not have done it, but the hula skirt and coconut bra sure did.)

MR EVANS ←

And there's more!

· Ran in hallway again.

· Reminded math teacher that when microwaves were invented, people no longer needed to make popcorn over a fire. Now we have calculators, so it won't be long before we don't need math teachers, either.

· Told lunch ladies that their macaroni and cheese smelled like the inside of an abandoned chicken coop.

· Ran in hallway AGAIN.

· And finally, got in an argument with Mr. Dover, our gym teacher, over doing laps. Isabella told him that we're not supposed to run in school.

Obviously she was taking advantage of my Aunt Carol's willingness to throw the teacher notes away, and just wants to see how much she can get away with. I didn't even want to bring it up with Aunt Carol tonight, because I'm embarrassed by Isabella. I'll talk to Isabella about it tomorrow and ask her to take it down a notch.

Isabella is a LAMB. I know she'll take it down a notch.

Wednesday 25

Dear Dumb Diary,

   Notchwise, Isabella only knows how to go up.

SQUOOSH

   I tried to explain to her that she is over-mining the natural resource of my Aunt Carol, and if she keeps at it, it's going to dry up. One day it might not be there when we really need it — like if we were to put Angeline in a locker and weld it shut accidentally. (Recently I learned how to weld on the Internet. Accidentally.)

Isabella doesn't care. She continued her crime spree throughout the day, and Miss Anderson even personally walked her down to the office one time herself.

I told her that if she kept at it, sooner or later she was going to get detention, and for a moment, I think I got through to her, because she stopped for a second and thought.

I wanted to apologize about Isabella to Aunt Carol tonight, but she's out on a date again, and Stinker still won't cut one. (I tried him on cabbage and broccoli tonight — he can't resist anything because mom's exquisite appetizers are driving him crazy.) He looks to me like he's starting to inflate a little.

Thursday 26

Dear Dumb Diary,

   Meat loaf. And not just meat loaf. Also, Angeline was at our table today. I had no idea why she decided to sit with Isabella and me, but Angeline can sit anywhere she wants. She is immune, it seems, to **The Rules of the Lunchroom Tables**. (There's a cool kid table, a jerk table, a computer kid table. . . . you get the picture.)

   Angeline sat down and all friendly and playful she goes, "Quite the little office romance, huh?"

   I didn't know what she was talking about so I said, "Yes."

   "Our assistant principal seems to be falling in love," she whispered.

Angeline
and
Meat Loaf

UCK.

Isabella said, "No duh. Miss Anderson is really coming on strong."

Angeline might have gagged a little, but school meat loaf has that effect on most people.

"Miss Anderson?" she said.

"Yeah," Isabella said. "I've been up there sixteen times in two days, and Miss Anderson is always up there hanging around, making excuses to go into Mr. Devon's office. She gave him Jamie's valentine. In fact, she acts just like Jamie does when she tries to talk to Hudson." (Hudson Rivers, you might recall Dumb Diary, is the eighth-cutest guy in my grade and **shut up, Isabella!**)

Then Angeline changed. I saw her wide blue eyes narrow. Her perfect nostrils flared into . . . into . . . well, they were still perfect, but they were somewhat less ladylike. And her eternal smile flattened a bit into what must have been a scowl, but like the scowl a Care Bear might give you.

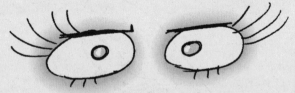

I was so happy. Can you believe how jealous she was that it was MY valentine that Miss Anderson had selected? I guess you haven't stolen my favorite teacher from me after all, hmmm, Angeline?

When I looked up, I realized that Bruntford had sidled up next to our table. Was she just doing her normal lunch patrol, or was she EAVESDROPPING? I wondered, although I didn't have to wonder long, because I saw her glare across the cafeteria at Miss Anderson who happened to be breezing through in an especially pretty manner.

Strangely, Isabella was looking at Miss Anderson with the exact same expression. I had no idea that two faces as different as theirs could even make the same expression.

The bell rang and we all broke up and I waited around for Isabella at her locker, but she never showed. Somebody told me that she got detention. This sugar withdrawal is really going badly for her.

Aunt Carol was gone again at dinner and I asked my mom if she was ever going to eat with us again, and she smiled and said that she thought Aunt Carol would be getting her own place to live very soon and she wouldn't be surprised if after the party tomorrow night, we saw even less of her.

It's more important than ever that I find out what's going on, and only Stinker can help me. I fed

him a can of beans and some frozen waffles after
dinner and I've explained to him how important
it is that he grosses up my room before bedtime.
Looking at the clock on the wall, he only has a
couple minutes to go, and it looks like this bloaty
little beagle is going to disobey me **AGAIN**.

FRONT

BACK

SIDE

TOP

ADMIT IT STINKER. YOU'RE FULL
OF GAS.

Friday 27

Dear Dumb Diary,

Isabella **DID** get detention yesterday. I told her there was a limit to what Aunt Carol could do with teachers' notes.

And speaking of teachers, my Aunt Carol's little get-together tonight caused actual teachers to be **HERE** in my actual house. I'm not kidding: **REAL TEACHERS**. It hadn't occurred to me that since Aunt Carol just started working at the school, it would be teachers and office ladies that would get herded through my private house.

Like an orangutan, you just don't expect to see A LIVE TEACHER IN YOUR HOUSE

I kid you not. Mr. Dover, the gym teacher (his real name is Ben Dover if you can handle it), was here. And not wearing a whistle or carrying a clipboard or telling anybody to hustle.

Miss Palmer, the science teacher, was here, wearing a dress that was actually kind of **FLATTERING**. I thought that was going to gross me out to write, but it didn't.

Mr. Evans was here, but his head vein wasn't. In many ways, he resembled a human being that didn't even have a big old ugly head vein.

The office ladies were here and they were not being mean at all, even though my mom was not handing out those little chocolate bars. I'm beginning to wonder if that one Mean Office Lady that we disabled was the one making them so grumpy. Maybe she was like an un-calming goat — like a goat that was always making its little collages all over their barnyard.

There must have been fifteen teachers in my house, including Mr. VanDoy, who still wasn't smiling, but at least he wasn't handing out social studies homework, either.

Then Assistant Principal Devon came in, and Aunt Carol, who I thought was not looking where she was going, slammed into him the way I crashed into Bruntford. Exactly — except for the huge . . .

I still can hardly believe it. It was one of those awesomely horrible types of kisses that is super gross and super excellent at the same time, like two people trying to chew one piece of gum at the same time. My aunt and Assistant Principal Devon **KISSED**.

Nice gusting!

We've always needed a word for things that are nice and disgusting at the same time.

And this is right about where Isabella came in, with Bruntford, (CAN YOU BELIEVE IT???) who, in this big friendly voice said, "Did we miss anything?" I looked at Isabella's hands and they were filthy. So were Bruntford's. I assumed that they had been wrestling, but Isabella took me into the bathroom and filled me in.

FILTH

FILTH

Isabella did get detention yesterday. Isabella said it only took a few minutes in the office before she could tell that Angeline had not been talking about Miss Anderson. She had been talking about my Aunt Carol. Isabella said it was totally obvious that Aunt Carol and Assistant Principal Devon really liked each other — which explains the big smooch — and that she overheard Aunt Carol talking about how **"special"** this party was going to be for her, and how she wished Miss Anderson wasn't going to be there.

Isabella said that all this lovey-dovey stuff was a very good thing, because it was working out so well for her personally.

EXCELLENT
← SPY WORK

I didn't understand. I mean, I got it that Aunt Carol didn't want Miss Anderson at the party flirting with her assistant principal, but why was Miss Anderson even interested? She could have dated Assistant Principal Devon anytime in the last five years. Why, all of a sudden, was she so interested now?

Miss Anderson is an expert at standing in pretty ways.

Isabella pointed at our identical shoes (the ones that make me look 20 or something). Then I remembered why Isabella bought them. She only bought them because I had them.

Miss Anderson was just like Isabella was with my shoes. Except the assistant principal is my shoes, and Aunt Carol is me, who had the shoes in the first place. Angeline doesn't really have a shoe role here. Anyway, Miss Anderson liked Assistant Principal Devon because Aunt Carol liked him.

Then Isabella confessed **WHY** it's working out so well for her personally. She's been getting in trouble on purpose for the candy. Every time she would go to the office, Aunt Carol would throw away the teacher's note, and Isabella would grab a handful of candy. Isabella was doing crime for chocolate. She knew I was right about the detention. But she wasn't trying to *avoid* it. She was trying to *get* it. She figured that if she got detention, she could spend an hour or so in the office eating as much chocolate as she wanted.

But as soon as she fully understood the situation, she needed to make sure that Miss Anderson couldn't break up her **ENDLESS CANDY SUPPLY** and that meant keeping her out of the picture. Besides, Miss Anderson had rejected her decorated padlock idea in favor of Angeline's collages and Isabella needed to get even for that, as well. (Remember? That's how she rolls. Oh man, I want a way to roll.)

Isabella was **not** going to give up her chocolate...

So this is why today, right after school, Isabella ran out to the parking lot, got down on her hands and knees, and crawled up to Miss Anderson's car. Her plan was to let the air out of one of the tires so she couldn't make it over to the party. But here's the thing: Bruntford was already there letting the air out herself.

Why? Right? I mean **WHY??** You know why? *You want to know why?* Isabella asked her why. And you know what she said? Because Aunt Carol is her friend. For whatever weird reason that friends like each other, the two of them just hit it off. It was **LIKE AT FIRST SIGHT.** Bruntford did it for her friend. And in that moment, she and Isabella were just . . . normal humans. They were two people who were enjoying a beautiful crime together. Bruntford even gave Isabella a ride over to my house.

SKIP   SKIP SKIP SKIP SKIP   SKIP SKIP

ALSO KIND OF **NICEGUSTING**

We came out of the bathroom just as Angeline was walking in. **INTO MY HOUSE.** And her hands were, probably for the first time ever, **dirty**. And what was Angeline doing here? And why were *her* hands dirty?

Fortunately, I had the assistant principal there to get to the bottom of things.

"Where were you, Angeline? Why are your hands so dirty?"

"I stopped to help Miss Anderson fix a flat on her car," she said. **OH, HO! THAT FIGURES!!!** Leave it to Angeline to help the enemy.

"So, uh, where is Miss Anderson?" Aunt Carol asked in a tone that suggested she hoped an escaped tiger was involved.

"I guess I wasn't much help," Angeline said.
"I lost the nuts, and we couldn't attach the spare
tire to the car. Miss Anderson apologized. She said
she would probably miss the party."

"Go wash your hands, Angeline," Mr. Devon
said. "I have a little announcement."

Notice
how the
dirt looks
a little cute
on her?

Isabella watched Angeline walk through my actual house, which was now full of actual teachers. When she got back, we found out what the little announcement was:

Assistant Principal Devon slid his hand around Aunt Carol's waist and said, "I'd like to introduce you all to the future Mrs. Devon. Carol and I are engaged."

Angeline went over and hugged Assistant Principal Devon and said:

"Congratulations, Uncle Dan."

UNCLE DAN?

Angeline is his **NIECE**? It all made sense. Angeline *knew* about this. She knew that I'm Aunt Carol's niece. **Does that mean we're related?** At the very least, we're co-nieces. Mom said nothing can get under your skin like a relative. So did Isabella. Angeline and I are now . . . cousins? Second cousins? Something like that. Anyway, Angeline will be my aunt's niece, as I am. Angeline knew all of this, and was taking some sort of sick delight in it — I just knew it.

My mom cried. Bruntford attempted **Gigglecide** against Isabella, and this time, it looked . . . *okay* for some reason. Like, it wasn't so weird seeing Bruntford happy.

The teachers clapped and laughed and raised their glasses. Angeline came and stood next to me and I think that she may have been doing it just to look clean and lovely and bright in comparison. From this moment on, I would never be able to be the clean and lovely and bright one. At best, all I can hope for is **SECOND FILTHIEST,** and **NOT THE DUMBEST.**

It was as though nobody on earth could fully grasp the tragedy of me being related to Angeline.

Except maybe Stinker, who chose this exact moment to sum up how I was feeling by walking into the living room and cutting the fart he had been baking for three weeks.

We had to run outside and watch through the windows as Stinker ate the incredibly delicious appetizers off everybody's plates. He had planned this all along. I just know it. Nobody was willing to go back into the house. Nobody could have. Well-played, Stinker, you pungent skunk-hound.

I thought Mom was going to totally freak out. She had been planning this party for so long and now all of her hard work was disappearing down the gullet of a beagle. But then somebody started laughing this loud, barking, out-of-control laughter that just makes you laugh when you hear it.

It was Mr. VanDoy. There was something about a house-clearing dog fart that finally got to him. Dog farts. That's right. That's what makes VanDoy smile. And laugh. And made everybody else — including my mom — laugh, which considering how much time she had spent on her appetizers, was pretty amazing.

I went over to congratulate my Aunt Carol. My heart wasn't in it, but she was so happy that I almost couldn't bring myself to say something mean about Angeline.

But I have a lot of willpower so I did anyway. "You know, Angeline was trying to help Miss Anderson get to your party today. That's pretty lousy, don't you think? Trying to wreck your special moment?" And Aunt Carol just laughed.

She said, "Jamie, the other day I was over at Dan's house, and Angeline changed the oil in my car. The girl knows her way around a wrench. If Angeline lost the nuts, she lost them on purpose."

Nuts

Then it became clear to me. Isabella and Miss Bruntford had slowed Miss Anderson down, but Angeline must have seen her changing the tire and knew she'd make it here and spoil this moment for my Aunt Carol. So Angeline pretended to help and she lost the nuts on purpose. She did it because she knows that Assistant Principal Devon and Aunt Carol belong together. She wasn't mad the other day that Miss Anderson had chosen my valentine, she was mad that Miss Anderson was butting in.

Although I still think she was partially motivated by being able to make me look bad. From now on I have to make sure that my gruesome little cousin attends all family functions so that I can carry him around like an accessory. That's got to help a little.

And his various colors of grime go with anything!

Eventually, Miss Anderson did stop by. She got a ride from the tow-truck guy that came to help her with her car. She talked and giggled with Assistant Principal Devon and Aunt Carol like nothing had ever happened. And since the tow-truck guy was a total hottie, Isabella says that Miss Anderson is not going to hold a grudge against us. And let's face it — Isabella is an expert on grudges.

I sat down on the porch and watched everybody mingle on the front lawn and laugh. And I remembered when Isabella and I were trying to figure out if adults could become human, and I finally realized that they couldn't.

But I also realized that humans can't become adults, either.

Here's how I see it: We all get mad, we all care about our friends, and we all have a selfish side. But animals have all those things, too. The difference is that we humans laugh about stuff, and we laugh like crazy. It was Mr. VanDoy that made me ask the question: Can adults become human? And it was Mr. VanDoy that helped me answer it. Here, tonight, at my house, everybody was a human. There were no adults.

So exactly what are adults and where do they come from? I have no idea, but I am pretty sure that I do not want to go there.

Who would have believed that a beagle fart could open your eyes and make them burn at the same time?

Thanks for listening, Dumb Diary.

Jamie Kelly

About Jim Benton

Jim Benton is not a middle-school girl, but do not hold that against him. He has managed to make a living out of being funny, anyway.

He is the creator of many licensed properties, some for big kids, some for little kids, and some for grown-ups who, frankly, are probably behaving like little kids.

You may already know his properties: It's Happy Bunny™ or Just Jimmy™, and you are about to get to know Dear Dumb Diary.

He's created a kids' TV series, designed clothing, and written books.

Jim Benton lives in Michigan with his spectacular wife and kids. They do not have a dog, and they especially do not have a vengeful beagle. This is his first series for Scholastic.

Jamie Kelly has no idea that Jim Benton, or you, or anybody is reading her diaries.